The circus was renamed "Dumbo's Flying Circus," and Dumbo traveled in a special streamlined car. But best of all, he forgave everyone who had been unkind to him, for his heart was as big as his magical ears.

The firemen brought a big net and held it out.

"Jump, my darling baby, jump!" shrieked the mother clown.

Dumbo jumped, but as he jumped the black feather slipped from his trunk and floated away. Now his magic was gone, and Dumbo plunged down like a stone.

"You can fly!" Timothy shouted frantically. "The feather's a fake. You can fly!"

Dumbo heard the shout and, doubtfully, spread his ears wide. Not two feet above the net he stopped his plunge and swooped up into the air!

A mighty gasp arose from the audience. They knew it couldn't be, but it was! *Dumbo was flying!*

While the crowd roared its delight, Dumbo did power dives, loops, spins, and barrel rolls. He swooped down to pick up peanuts and squirted a trunkful of water on the clowns.

The keepers freed Mrs. Jumbo and brought her to the tent in triumph to see her baby fly. So all of Dumbo's worries had come to an end.

By evening, Dumbo was a hero from coast to coast.

Timothy became Dumbo's manager, and he saw to it that Dumbo got a wonderful contract with a big salary and a pension for his mother.

Timothy shouted, "We must keep your flying a secret—a surprise for your act in this afternoon's show."

No one noticed Dumbo when he and Timothy came quietly back. It was already time for Dumbo to get into his costume. Inside the walls of the cardboard house he had to wait all through the show until fire crackled up around him.

At last Timothy leaned down and handed him the feather. "In just a second, Dumbo," he whispered, "you'll be the most famous animal in all the world!"

Cr . . . rr . . . rr . . . ack! Cr . . . rr . . . rr . . . ack! crackled the fire. The clown act was on! Flames shot up around the cardboard house. Clang! Clang! roared the clown fire engine, rushing toward the blaze.

From the far end of the ring, a redheaded mother clown came running. "Save my baby!" she screamed. "He's on the top floor!"

"Here, take this . . . tell the baby elephant it's a *magic* feather. Tell him if he holds it, he can fly." The boss crow winked and flew off.

Timothy handed Dumbo the feather and scurried up his trunk to the brim of his cap.

The trick worked like a charm. The very instant that Dumbo wrapped the tip of his trunk around the feather, flap . . . flap . . . flap! went his ears. Up into the air he soared like a bird! Over the tallest treetops he sailed. He glided, he dipped, he dived. Three times he circled over the heads of the cheering crows. Then he headed back to the circus grounds.

He grabbed one of Dumbo's wet ears and patted it. "You won't be a clown anymore. You'll be famous . . . the only flying elephant in the whole wide world!"

And Timothy and Dumbo began all over again to practice flying.

But it wasn't easy. Time after time, Dumbo tried to take off. Time after time, he sprawled out flat on his face. Soon the crows began to feel sorry for the little fellow. When Timothy told them all the sad things that had happened to Dumbo because of his big ears, they flew down and offered to help.

One of the crows took Timothy aside. "Flying's just like swimming," he whispered. "It's just a matter of believing that you can do it." He turned and snatched a long, black feather from his tail.

When the morning sun arose, Timothy was the first to awaken. He blinked and looked up. Just above him, four old black crows sat and stared at him.

"Why . . . why . . . ," yawned Timothy, rubbing his eyes. "Where am I?"

"You're up in our tree," snapped the crows crossly. "That's where you are."

"*Tree?*" gasped Timothy. He looked around. Sure enough, there he was, sitting on a branch. He and Dumbo *were* up in a tree! The ground was far, far below. "But . . . but . . . how did we get here?" he stammered.

"*How!*" cackled the crows. "You and that elephant just came a-flyin' up!"

"Flying!" Timothy yelled. "Dumbo, Dumbo, wake up! Dumbo, we're up in a tree! You FLEW here!"

Slowly Dumbo opened his eyes. He glanced down. He gulped. Then he struggled to his feet. But suddenly he slipped on the smooth tree bark and fell. Down . . . down . . . down! He bounced from branch to branch, with Timothy clinging to his trunk. Plonk! They landed in a shallow pond just underneath the tree. The crows chuckled and cawed from above.

Timothy scrambled up out of the water and wrung out Dumbo's tail. "Dumbo," he panted. "You can fly! If you can fly when you're asleep, you can fly when you're awake. Your ears, Dumbo, they're your fortune!"

He stretched out his wings and flapped them, 1-2-3-4. But hard as he tried, Dumbo could not leave the ground.

At last, almost too tired to stand, the two friends gave up and started gloomily back toward the sleeping circus.

"Don't worry, Dumbo," Timothy whispered as he curled up on Dumbo's hat brim for a good night's sleep. "We'll have you flying yet!"

So Dumbo fell asleep with a tired smile on his face and a beautiful dream in his heart. In the dream he was flying as easily and gracefully as a bird–soaring through the air, high above the circus. It was a wonderful dream, and it seemed very real to Dumbo.

Mother Jumbo listened sympathetically, stroking him gently with her trunk.

"Don't you worry, Baby," she told him. "You're having a hard time now, and I'm sorry I can't be with you to help. But just remember always to do your best and, as Timothy says, you'll soon be flying high."

Then sadly they said good night, and Timothy and Dumbo continued on their way. Out on the bare fields in the starlight they went to work.

With Timothy as teacher Dumbo practiced running and jumping and hopping.

Hidden in a pile of hay was Timothy Mouse, the smallest animal with the circus.

"They can't treat the little fellow that way," he muttered. "Not while Timothy Mouse is around."

"Hey there, little fellow!" he called to Dumbo. "Don't be afraid. I'm your friend. I want to help you."

Timothy ran up toward Dumbo's ear. "We'll get your mother out of jail, you and I together, and we'll make you the star of the show. You'll be flying high!

"Say!" he went on, staring at Dumbo's ears. "Those ears are as good as wings. I'll teach you to fly!"

Quietly Dumbo crept out of the tent with Timothy, and soon they came to the prison car on a siding.

Dumbo told his mother all about the clown act, and how unhappy he was without her, and about the wonderful idea Timothy had for making him a success.

A gang of noisy boys came pushing in first for the afternoon show. "We want to see the elephant," they yelled, "–the one with the sailboat ears!"

"Look . . . there he is."

A boy grabbed one of Dumbo's ears and pulled it hard. Then he made an ugly face and stuck out his tongue.

Mrs. Jumbo couldn't stand it. She snatched the boy up with her trunk and spanked him, hard.

"Help!" he cried. "Help! Help!"

"What's going on here?" cried the ringmaster, rushing forward with his whip. "Tie her down!" he yelled.

Soon she was behind the bars in the prison wagon with a big sign that said: "Danger! Mad Elephant! Keep Out!"

The next day, they made Dumbo into a clown. They painted his face with a foolish grin and dressed him in a baby dress. On his head they put a bonnet. They used him in the most ridiculous act in the show– a make-believe fire. Every night he had to jump from the top of a blazing cardboard house, down into a firemen's net. The audience thought it a great joke. But Dumbo felt disgraced.

"He's a disgrace to us," the big animals agreed, and they turned their backs on him.

Sadly, Dumbo toddled behind his mother, with his trunk clasped to her tail. He tried to hurry along faster so he wouldn't hear the laughter, but he stumbled. He tripped over his ears. Down he splashed into a puddle of mud. Now the crowds laughed even louder. Mrs. Jumbo scowled at them. She picked Dumbo up and carried him in her trunk the rest of the way.

When the parade finally came back to the tent, everyone hustled to get ready for the afternoon show. Mrs. Jumbo put Dumbo in her wooden bathtub, and as she scrubbed she whispered comforting words.

By morning the rain had stopped, the tent was all set up, and the circus was busy getting ready for the big parade. The band played. Everyone fell in line.

Then off pranced the gay procession down the main street. There were creamy-white horses, licorice-colored seals! There were lady acrobats in pink silk tights, lions pacing in their gilded wagon-cages, elephants marching with slow, even steps.

The crowds on the sidewalk cheered. Then, suddenly, their eyes opened wide. They craned their necks. "Look . . . look!" they cried. "Look at that silly animal with the draggy ears! He *can't* be an elephant . . . he must be a clown!"

They lighted torches and stuck them in the ground.
Men and animals came bustling out of the train into
the windy, wet night. Mrs. Jumbo worked with the
others, and her baby helped a little.

It was dark when he pulled into the station. Rain poured down hard, but the circus began to unload. The roustabouts jumped down from the freight cars.

"All aboard!" shouted the ringmaster.

The acrobats, the jugglers, the tumblers, the snake charmers scrambled to their places on the train. The keepers locked the animal cages. Then with a jiggety jerk and a brisk puff-puff, off sped Casey Jones! The circus was on its way!

Everyone was singing. Everyone was happy.

Happiest of all was Mrs. Jumbo, for in her stall was a chubby, brand-new baby elephant. Though the other animals called the baby Dumbo, his mother loved him dearly. Even though his ears *were* big.

All night, while the baby animals slept, Casey Jones whistled and puffed, hauling the long train to the city where the circus was to open its show.

It was spring . . . spring in the circus!

After the long winter's rest, it was time to set out again on the open road.

"Toot! Toot!" whistled Casey Jones, the locomotive of the circus train.

Library of Congress Control Number: 2004100449
ISBN: 0-7364-2309-5
www.goldenbooks.com
First Random House Edition 2004
Printed in the United States of America 20 19 18 17 16 15

Walt Disney's

DUMBO

Illustrated by the Walt Disney Studio

 A GOLDEN BOOK • NEW YORK